D0046332

S						
1						
8	9	10	11	12	13	14
15	16	17	18	19	20	21
22	23	24	25	26	27	28

APRIL

S	M	T	W	T	F	S
			1	2	3	4
5	6	7	8	9	10	11
12	13	14	15	16	17	18
19	20	21	22	23	24	25
26	27	28	29	30		

JUNE

S	M	T	W	T	F	S
	1	2	3	4	5	6
7	8	9	10	11	12	13
14	15	16	17	18	19	20
21	22	23	24	25	26	27
28	29	30				

CONTENTS

The Fireside Book

A picture and a poem
for every mood
chosen by

David Hope

Printed and published by
D.C. THOMSON & CO., LTD.,
185 Fleet Street, LONDON EC4A 2HS.
© D.C. Thomson & Co., Ltd., 1997.
ISBN 0-85116-648-2

THE VISITOR

SHE comes to stay for just two weeks
   She makes the place her own.
She brings some biscuits and a dish
And food for her alone.
She rushes up and down the stairs
And calls out in the dark,
The only visitor we have
Who's up before the lark!

She doesn't like the front door bell
She doesn't like the phone,
And, sometimes, when she sees TV,
She gives a little groan.
When she goes home we breathe a sigh
And never make a fuss,
Perhaps you guessed — our daughter's cat
Has been to stay with us!

Iris Hesselden

MY FEATHERED FRIENDS

THE chirpy sparrow stays with us though skies be grey or blue,
   Through coldest of our Winter days he stays forever true;
n my tall hedgerow bright eyes peep — I'm sure they know my voice,
And for the crumbs I scatter t'would seem that they rejoice.

hey may not have bright plumage like some other birds we know,
But still dark greys and browns can shimmer in the sunlight's glow;
Each morning as they call to me I feel my spirits rise,
nfused with joy that lifts their tiny wings up to the skies.

Georgina Hall

BREATH OF WINTER

FROZEN, the falls where April's flood
   Surged down with echoes loud.
The sombre crags like witches brood
In ragged shawls of cloud.

Huddled, the sheep, and half-asleep
The cattle in the byre.
The crofters close their doors, and heap
Fresh peats upon the fire.

Bitter the wind that lifts the spray
Where western tides run high;
Only the gulls seek silver prey
Beneath the wintry sky.

Patient, the hills. They do not sleep
When crimson sun sinks low,
But draw their forests round their feet
And wait the coming snow.

Brenda G. Macrow

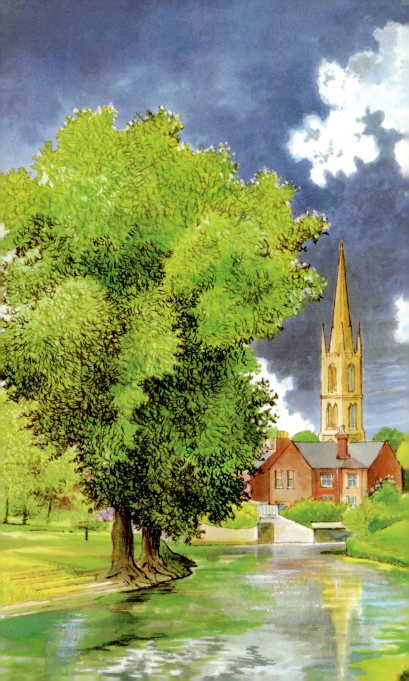

GRANTHAM

I SEE you yet, small valley town,
  With one pale steeple lifting
To quell the storm cloud's sullen frown,
And it so slowly drifting.

I hear you now, St Wulfram's bells,
On windy nights loud ringing.
Your passioned music wildly swells
And wakes my heart to singing.

I know you still, sweet Witham stream,
As slender as a maiden.
You ripple softly through my dream
With memories over-laden.

I said farewell, old valley town,
One cold and sad December.
A shooting star came tumbling down:
How well I can remember!

Peter Cliffe

SONG: O MARY MACNEIL

O Mary MacNeil, are your sad thoughts far roaming
Over the ocean, across the dark land;
O Mary MacNeil, do you dream of the foaming,
The white manes of sea, the white acres of sand?
And what is the prayer on your lips when you waken
Into a world that is fickle and vain?
O Mary MacNeil, did you think you had taken
The weed-clustered path to the clachan again?

O Mary MacNeil, is the tang of peat reeking
More sweet in your nostrils than powder and scent:
And what is the whisper your tired ears are seeking
And where are your wandering glances out-bent?
O is it the mouths of the wind to caress you,
Gentler than lover and kinder than rain;
O Mary MacNeil, does the vision still bless you
Of the path to the thatch-covered clachan again?

O Mary MacNeil, from the surge of the city,
Does there rise up before you the Mountain, a shape
Soft as death, a green shrine; and do you ever pity
Yourself, a lost prisoner seeking escape:
Escape from the corrie of buildings and bustle,
Escape from the fetters of yearning, of pain:
O Mary MacNeil, are you hearing the rustle
Of birds in the eaves of the clachan again?

O Mary MacNeil, the grey wind is still maund'ring
With old Gaelic songs mingled up in its breath:
But Mary MacNeil, every day you are wand'ring
A dream nearer home — and a night nearer death.
The waters are waiting, the distance is calling;
Embark, steer your cargo of life to the West,
And, Mary MacNeil, when the cool dusk is falling,
Set your heart free again on the Isles of the Blest.

R.L. Cook

HOME THOUGHTS FROM BARBADOS

ON Paradise Heights the woods are green,
   Jungle-green and starred with flowers;
Casuarina sweeps the sky,
Hibiscus, bougainvillea bowers
Drenched in sun. Beyond the palms
Pale waves of glass on coral white,
And dappled shade; trade winds and mangoes,
Mindless days, and ocean beating bright.

I see frail snowdrops in the ditch,
Timid jasmine's golden show,
Beech tracery, black twiggy oak,
Starving fieldfares in the snow;
Sheltering cattle at the dyke,
Sun yet too timorous to be gay,
And o'er the expectant February land
The grey, uncertain skies of Galloway.

Alan Temperley

SORRY

I'M sorry, my dear
  But I rather fear
You'll have to make supper tonight —
Please don't let it burn
Yes, I know it's my turn
But sadly, I have to sit tight.

I'm lazy? Oh no
I've got plenty of go,
I'd be on my feet like a shot —
And I'm supple and fit
When it comes to the bit
So it isn't rheumatics I've got.

It's just your bad luck
That I'm currently stuck
But my dearest, I'm sure you agree —
It wouldn't be fair
To rise from my chair
When pussy's asleep on my knee!

Alison Mary Fitt

THE DAY THAT WAS

WHEN the dreary days of Winter
　Are shadows borne away,
A tender longing calls me
To that little, Highland bay,
For the sighing in the grasses
And the calling of the sea
Are the whispers and the voices
Of a day that used to be.

And I'll take the quiet pathway
That meanders to the cove,
Breathe the thyme and myrtle,
Scents of heaven that I love,
And the ocean will be waiting
Like a lost and longed-for thing,
White-crested, foaming shoreward,
Sapphire blue and glittering.

And the wild wind rushing landward,
Unchanged and hauntingly
Will sing the sweet-sad music
Of the day that used to be,
And the crying of the seabirds,
And the calling of the sea
Will awake the joyful laughter
Of the girl that once was me.

Eileen Melrose.

OH, AVALON!

LONG, long ago in time forgot,
　When men were bold and ladies fair,
There lived a knight named Lancelot
Who loved a lass called Guinevere.

But Guinevere, alas, was wed
To Arthur, who was Lance's king,
And yet they sinned, or so 'tis said,
One sunny evening in the Spring.

Now Mordred was a jealous lad
Who nursed wild hopes of Arthur's crown.
He proved poor Guinevere was bad
And got young Lance thrown out of town.

So Lance went off, where no man knew,
And Guinevere became a nun.
It left King Arthur feeling blue,
While Mordred's day was nearly done.

It's just an old, romantic play
Of love and battles, lost and won
And people (much like us today),
Back in the time of Avalon.

Peter Cliffe

DRY-STONE DYKERS

WIND tormented moorland
  dykes
Bravely built by weathered
  hand,
Curving over hill and moor,
Monuments to a departed band.

Firmly meshing earth and sky,
Defying nature's surging scorn,
Obdurate, unblessed by priest,
Standing Stones in prosaic
  form.

Hardy souls these dry-stone
  builders,
Hefting rocks to fit together,
Cursing rain and chill
  and shiver,
Giving thanks for softer
  weather.

Pausing now to ease the strain,
Skyward glancing, lifting cap,
Watching the buzzard's
  circling flight
While pipits pipe and
  stonechats tap.

Taking heed of heaven's
  moods —
Changing pageant of
  the weather;
Tasting pervasive earthy
  scents
Distilled by sun and rain
  together.

And cart by cart the horses
  come
Urged on by oath and touch
  of leather,
Then spilling broken virgin rock
In cairns to challenge brawn
  and labour.

Yard by yard, slowly stretching,
This crafted work of rugged
  splendour
Will stand a century and more,
A rustic sculpture in nature
  blended.

Now time has touched those
  lonely dykes
With moss and lichen's
  gentle plying;
And frequently a weasel peeps
At sheltering sheep snugly
  lying.

No voices now, no stir,
  no chatter,
The stones that echoed to
  their laughter
Still hear the lark and linnet
  singing
While the buzzard circles
  slowly skyward.

Jim Carnduff

WAITING

SLOWLY, slowly comes the Spring,
Here a little, there a sign,
Now a glimpse from deeps of gloom,
Now a gleam whole hours long,
Inch by inch and weeks between:
Slowly comes the Spring.

Snowdrop 'neath the dripping hedge,
Crocus lifting through the rime,
Rowan dreaming by the gate,
Almond weary for the call;
Trees and grass and buds asleep,
Earth and sky grey-bound and sad:
Waiting for the Spring.

Gnats a-dance in sun-warmed path,
Sparrow chirping on the thorn,
Spider on the southern wall,
Thrush and robin in the mirk
Lifting up their faithful hearts:
Calling for the Spring.

Slowly — but slowly — comes the Spring,
Ah, but always sure it comes,
Slowly — slowly — sure it comes!
Lo, one morn you wake and know,
As the thrush and sparrow know,
As the buds and flowers know,
In your blood and heart and brain,
In the sunrise of your soul,
That the miracle is wrought.
See it. Feel it. Live it now.
Spring — Spring — Spring is here!

Shan Bullock

MA PETITE

"SING a song of nothing,"
   So the prattler said;
"Nothing? Bless your little soul,
Why nothing's in your head!

"Come and let me tap it, dear,
'Twixt curl and golden curl:
Empty, empty: what a head
For a little girl.

"Perhaps it's not so empty though;
Daddy's such a quiz:
Isn't all the world inside,
Everything that is.

"Rainbows in the afternoon,
Butterflies with wings,
Tiger Tom, the pussy cat,
And hosts of other things.

"Christmas pies and hooks and eyes,
Chocolates and cakes,
And dreams, O lovely dreams, that go
When girlie laughing wakes."

"Well, now," said she and looked at me,
"This is a song to sing:
There's nothing, nothing, in my head,
And yet there's everything."

With that she skipped and laughed with glee
As only children can,
And then she said quite soberly,
"You are a funny man!"

Latimer McInnes

WHEN . . .

WHEN golden sun-shafts split the sky,
And clouds of birds go scudding by;

When bearded boughs are shaven clean,
And buds of hawthorn lather green;

When violets and celandines
Embroider lanes with Spring designs;

When drops of water, fresh-brewed, fall,
And thirsty meadows drink them all;

When streamlets flow like liquid glass,
And lambs bob up in seas of grass;

When dawn breaks out — a rash of light —
And feverish larks infect the night;

When Life wakes, wide-eyed, after rest,
Of all the seasons that's the best!

Glynfab John

REMEMBERING YOU

THE daffodils were beautiful —
And I remembered you.
The blackbird sang in the early light —
Did he remember, too?
The wind blew fresh and the sun grew bright
As it sparkled on the sea,
I thought of you, remembered you,
And how things used to be.
The clouds were low on the distant hills
And rain came falling fast,
But still my thoughts returned to you
With mem'ries of the past.
The Springtime weaves her magic spell
Through all I see and do,
But I'll keep Springtime in my heart,
For I remember you.

Iris Hesselden

HARESFIELD

UP to Haresfield's golden crest,
   Sun-caress't,
Where like scattered drifts of snow,
Every hawthorn in the glade
Throws her shade
On a cooler world below.

Hark, how from the heart of Spring,
Cuckoos sing
Now: and now: a bell-clear chime!
Bees with drumming fill the air,
Feasting there
Fiercely in the scented thyme.

And the larks! The joy they make;
How they shake
Notes from Heaven as clear as dew,
On the singing copse beneath:
We shall breathe
Music, love, this long day through.

Kenneth Hare

FAIRYLAND

I CHANCED upon a bluebell glade,
As I strolled in the glen;
A field of dreams before me lay;
I stopped a while — and then —

There came soft music round about,
Like birdsong at the dawn;
A stranger stood before my gaze —
He was a leprechaun!

He pranced and piped his tiny flute,
His feet were light and free;
Said he in little manly voice —
Will you come dance with me?

He danced me o'er the haze of blue,
Across the coral strand,
Far over the hill he danced me —
Away to Fairyland.

O lovely, mystic Fairyland!
Ne'er found but by the few,
Your little happy, dancing folk,
Will lure me back to you.

Something stirred in the bluebell glade,
And waked me at the dawn;
But I had been to Fairyland,
Danced with a leprechaun!

If you would go to Fairyland,
('Tis beautiful I swear),
Find you a little leprechaun,
And he will take you there.

Patricia McGavock

REBECCA DANCING

WITH flying hoofs and tossing manes
   I once spied playful ponies prancing,
A sweeter sight had never been
Until I saw Rebecca dancing.

Small head held high, dark eyes aglow
She was a picture so entrancing,
That everybody turned to gaze
Spellbound by Rebecca's dancing.

Pointing her toes she held her skirts
Lightly skipped whilst shyly glancing,
And bestowing smiles on all who watched
Enchanted by Rebecca's dancing.

On dark days at my lowest ebb
The Autumn of my life advancing,
Springtime fills my heart anew
When I recall Rebecca dancing.

Kathleen Corbitt

THE RAINBOW

IT'S been raining half the day
   But plodding wetly on my way
I see a graceful coloured arc
Curved high above the puddled park.

Red, yellow, orange, indigo
All set the greyish sky aglow —
And staring up from sodden shoes
I marvel at its merging hues.

Over the rainbow skies are blue
And happiness waits for me and you
They say — but getting there's the thing —
All fine for bluebirds on the wing!

And then there is a pot of gold
At Rainbow's End, or so we're told —
But nobody has ever found
The spot where rainbows touch the ground.

So I am quite content to know
The promise of that perfect bow —
The rain will surely stop and then —
Is that the sun I see again?

Alison Mary Fitt

HELTER-SKELTER

WE walked together by the sea
And watched the sunlight dance,
The sands of time were running fast
And life was all romance.
We walked together in the rain
And, laughing, ran for shelter,
The rainbow just above our heads
On youth's bright helter-skelter.

So now my thoughts go wandering
Recalling happy years,
The Summer walks, the Winter nights,
The laughter and the tears.
But all the love you ever gave
Will still provide my shelter,
And you will light my way each day
Around the helter-skelter.

Iris Hesselden

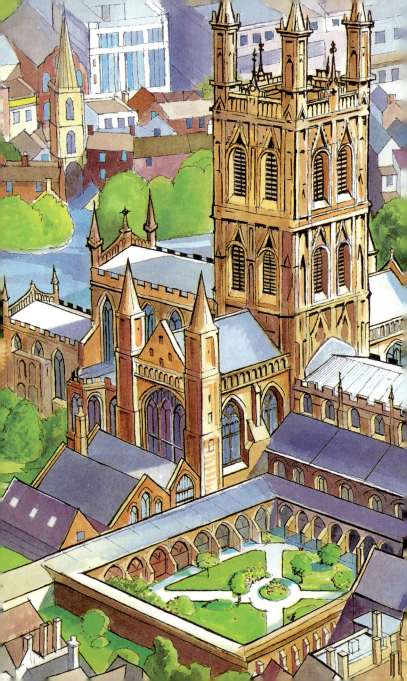

THE CLOISTERS — GLOUCESTER CATHEDRAL

THE cloister garth lies
   peaceful —
There's sun and shadow there,
As modern pilgrims take
   their ease
And offer up a prayer.

The ancient walls surround them,
Once built by men long dead,
And where they sit the monks
   once walked
With bowed and lowly head.

And where the gravelled walkways
And grassy turf hold sway
Mayhap they worked their plots
   of herbs
On some past, sunny day.

And did they tend some roses red,
Like those we see today,
Enjoy their hue and fragrance
While pausing on their way?

Their spirit hovers over us
Within this hallowed place,
And visits every pilgrim heart
With thoughts of peace and grace.

The chimes ring out the
   passing hour,
'Tis time to take our leave,
But we've been granted this
   brief time
Of joy and of reprieve.

Joan E. Selwyn

VAGABOND

A VAGABOND I like to be,
It is the only life for me —
The sky above, the earth below,
And all that Nature can bestow.

On cloudless nights the stars I see,
And each one seems to wink at me;
By day the sun, that orb so bright,
Befriends me with its warmth and light.

While far away from human din,
Wild creatures are to me like kin;
I soundly sleep in ruined barns,
And wash my face in ice-cold tarns.

I climb the hills, I roam the vales,
And tramp the lonely lanes of Wales;
I have my knapsack on my back,
Little I own yet nothing lack.

I drink from springs my thirst to slake,
And of my frugal fare partake:
After a meal of bread and cheese
I am content and feel at ease.

I would not swap my vagrant life
For cheerful hearth and caring wife;
I wish for neither fame nor wealth,
Just freedom outdoors and good health.

Glynfab John

SPRING FEVER

WHEN April dances down the lane
And every greening branch is shaken
By fitful breezes, once again
I feel my vagrant soul awaken.

When May lays garlands at my feet
And nesting birds call loud and shrill,
I hear a summons, wild and sweet,
That I must answer, come what will.

When June sings love songs from the stream,
And fleecy clouds drift high above,
You beckon me in every dream,
And I am coming, land I love.

Peter Cliffe

THE WINDOW

THE water coming in among the stone toes of the Hebrides,
   Atlantic water, somewhere between green and blue
Light like a gem.

All afternoon we pushed ankle-deep through low tide;
Crabs climbed carefully across a white silence,
Flounders boomed away in puffs of sand.

And far away, out towards Ireland,
Gannets drummed into the sea, plume on plume,
Deep into a shoal of herring.

And I was laughing all the time,
Scuffing water with my feet and laughing
In the stained-glass window of the summer.

Kenneth C. Steven

TOMORROW'S PROMISE . . .

THROUGH the rustling leaves of Summertime,
The breezes gently sigh,
And the chuckling brook is busy now
Splashing its way nearby!
The old stone bridge is seasoned through
The years of sun and rain,
And it's pleasant here to linger on
As daylight's on the wane.
The scent of sweetbriar fills the air
Which from the heat of day,
Now settles down to evening's cool,
Where here content, we'll stay
For just a few more moments yet,
To watch the cloudless sky
And guess tomorrow's forecast shows
Another fair day's nigh!

Elizabeth Gozney

A NIGHT IN JUNE

THE sun has long been set,
　　The stars are out by twos and threes,
The little birds are piping yet
Among the bushes and the trees;
There's a cuckoo, and one or two thrushes,
And a far-off wind that rushes,
And a sound of water gushes,
And the cuckoo's sovereign cry
Fills all the hollow of the sky.
Who would go 'parading'
In London, 'and masquerading',
On such a night of June
With that beautiful soft half-moon,
And all these innocent blisses?
On such a night as this is!

William Wordsworth

THE FIDDLER AT
THE GATE

THROUGH medieval streets I heard its
   Call, above the bustling throng,
The music danced around me,
A rhapsody of song.

The lilting airs they drew me —
Drew me as if to fate,
And I sought and found the fiddler
At the old Lincoln gate.

His looks were dark and foreign,
Eyes smouldered from his face
But from his burnished fiddle —
Notes delicate as lace.

To the Russian Steppes he took me,
To Vienna and to Rome,
To mountains and arid plains
Of minarets and dome.

I danced with fire and passion,
I was a gypsy queen,
I swayed with wild emotions,
I longed for sights unseen.

Bewitched — I have forsaken life
For dreams and I must stay
With the fiddler and his music
That holds me in its sway.

Kathryn L. Garrod

UPSTAIRS ON THE BUS

WHEN I ride upstairs on the bus
    I nearly touch the sky,
I see the birds hide in the trees
And watch the clouds go by.
Mum tells me, "Don't fall down the steps
And sit still on the seat,"
But Grandma smiles and sits up close
And gives me things to eat.
There's lots and lots of chimney pots
In rows all over town,
But we look over garden walls
To where the hills come down.
We keep on stopping, here and there,
But we've so much to see,
I like it upstairs on the bus,
When there's just Gran and me.

Iris Hesselden

THE PATCHWORK QUILT

SHE mixes blue and mauve and green,
  Purple and orange, white and red,
And all the colours in between
To patch a cover for her bed.

Oblong, triangle, star and square,
Oval, and round, she makes them fit
Into a wondrous medley there,
Colour by colour, bit by bit.

Over her knee it swiftly flows,
And round her feet, a bright cascade,
While at her touch it grows and grows,
Until at last the quilt is made.

And then across the bed it lies,
A thing of gorgeous crazy bloom,
As if a rainbow from the skies
Had shattered in her little room.

Elizabeth Fleming

MULL

I WENT to watch for otters
On a June night,
All the Hebrides going down lit
In the last molten embers of the sun.
I crouched in rocks away beyond
The glass rubbing of the sea.
It was so still you could have heard
A pin in Moscow;
Just the midges smudging round my head,
And a sheep bleating from terribly far
Its cry like a child's.
An eider ruddered out through deep seaweed
And somewhere else, a bird scuttered in to land.
But there was not the quickest whisker of otter
All along the length of that vast shore,
Just the moon rising behind, slow and breathless —
A ball of cobwebs.

Kenneth C. Steven

WINDSURFERS

LIKE birds of paradise they fly,
　Tacking the wind to tame the sea,
Winged warriors, straight and lithe of limb,
Their world young, awaiting, free.

Bright rainbow hues coast riffling waves,
Dip and rise with practised ease,
Wheel and race past, jet propelled,
Caught and thrust on Summer's breeze.

From sunset skies of beaten gold,
Shadowed silhouettes skim to shore,
Lash slapping sails to rusting cars,
Echoes their laughter — slamming door.

Fly, carefree bird of youth, take wing,
Follow your star, chart well your schemes
For as you sail the sea of life,
The wind of time steals hopes and dreams.

Kathryn L. Garrod

SUMMER MAGIC

MY little old walled garden
Has a sundial on the lawn,
And from there the blackbirds wake me
With their hymn to greet the dawn.

Throwing wide the casement window,
I lean out to view the day,
And a breeze that stirs the curtains
Brings the scent of new-mown hay.

Then the siren voice of Summer,
Ah! how sweetly she can sing,
Tells of glades where mocks the cuckoo,
And of swallows on the wing.

"Lie-abed, why do you linger?
There is magic in the morn.
Hide yourself beside the river:
You may glimpse the unicorn."

So, it's coffee, toast and marmalade,
Then off along the lane,
For the winding roads are calling,
And they shall not call in vain.

Peter Cliffe

SUMMER PILGRIMAGE

I CAME to the eternal hills,
  As one who sought a shrine,
The rock my "scallop shell of quiet",
My staff the towering pine.

My pilgrim-hat the curl of mist
That crowned the mountain's crest;
A ray of sunlight on the stream
The badge upon my breast.

My palmer's pouch the folded moor,
My psalm the waters loud,
My nomad shoes the shifting screes,
My cloak the mantling cloud.

I came, world-weary, to the hills
And, shedding all my care,
A token won of Summer's gold,
And found a blessing there.

Brenda G. Macrow

REFLECTIONS

FOLLOW the sound of the birdsong's echo,
Skimming the trees in a carefree way,
Season of joy in this Summer zenith,
Scenting the air, on this sun-filled day.

Murmuring bees seek the wine-filled nectar,
Shadows of birds trace sunlit heights;
Sweet, the fragrance on the breezes,
Coasting birds in their graceful flights.

Gently the raindrops' dimpling spatter,
Briefly amid the sunbeam's gold;
Blending the tints of the fragile rainbow,
Beauty in pastels, to unfold.

Later, the heat in sultry splendour,
Later, the roses full-blown sway;
Special for now is the month that lingers —
Special, this heaven-scent Summer's day!

Elizabeth Gozney

THE CALL OF THE BAND

SEE a silver band stride with spirit and pride
And smart as a whip down a street;
Cutting a dash as the cymbals clash
To the marching beat of its feet.

With a stirring tattoo, it paces to view;
Trumpets swell and the drummers roll
A military air with a rousing fanfare
That quickens the heart and soul.

Polished like glass, trombones gleam as brass
Fired in the gold of the sun;
Swinging high and low as the trumpets blow
For old battles lost and won.

The romance of a band by the sea and sand
With a cornet trembling sweet
As prayer soaring high to a rose-blushed sky,
In the evening's fading heat.

Our silver band's call to the civic hall,
Town carnivals and church fêtes,
To follow along and march with its song
That catches and captivates.

Kathryn L. Garrod

BALLAD

OH, a tired young clerk in days of old
   Met up with a gipsy girl.
Her eyes were bright, her smile was bold,
And she set his heart in a whirl.

"Girl, I want none of your paper flowers,
But I must tell you this:
I shall dream of you through the lonely hours,
So what must I pay for a kiss?"

Though she laughed at him, her look was kind,
And she answered him full and fair:
"You may take your kiss, and I shall not mind,
But the life that I live you'll share."

He knows no more the grim, grey town,
And the gipsy lass is his bride.
She sits by his side in her russet gown,
And they go where the gipsies ride.

Peter Cliffe

THE THOROUGHBRED

AS the afternoon sun blazes down,
  And dapples the handsome bay's dark brown,
Cool in the shade of a chestnut tree,
The thoroughbred stands there patiently,
His tail swishing at occasional flies
That buzz about his satiny thighs.

His sculptured head, with sensitive face
And wide-set eyes, portrays equine grace:
Flanks well groomed, shanks of muscle and bone,
Softly gleam, and with mane and tail tone;
Arabian sires endowed his breed
With spirit, stamina — and with speed.

Fleet-footed creature, renowned for his pace,
For sport he was bred, and trained to race;
An elegant horse with natural poise,
He hardly moves, and makes not a noise,
Yet many triumphs earned him such fame
That soon he became a household name.

Arab forebears still course through the blood
Of this living legend, now at stud;
Once champion supreme, tall he stands,
A long-legged stallion, of sixteen hands,
And from his hindquarters to his head
He's every inch a thoroughbred.

Glynfab John

OUR CATHY AND ME

IT'S a lovely day for the seaside,
   To play down by the sea,
We'll take our spades and buckets,
Build castles, our Cathy and me.

We'll look for crabs and treasure,
Left by the outgoing tide,
Collect some shells and seaweed,
And go for a long donkey ride.

We'll go down to the shoreline and paddle,
And watch Mr Punch in his show,
Buy Granny some shrimps with our pennies,
And ice-cream and lollies, you know.

We'll keep on playing till bedtime,
Then tired and sleepy we'll be,
We'll go home and dream of sandcastles,
That we've built, our Cathy and me.

Thomas H. Green

HILL FARM

THERE was a hill farm
   When we were young:
Its green fields
Small and stony
Hacked from the heather
Bloomed in the sun.

Heavy horses had soft white noses
Smelling of sorrel and sweet clover;
The curlews' trembling cries
Shivered over the moor and the mountain hare
And the piping of the golden plover.

We rode our round-table-backed steeds
Through the secret country of our urchin days
Crowned with gold pollen
Of birch and alder.

Now the farm is gone,
The fields are dry and brittle,
The sweated acres
Succumbing to the lusty heath;
The gaping roof has lost its slates, blown
Like leaves in the wind's breath.

Birch and alder still lean
Across the burn,
And the rain which once filled
Large hoof-prints to the brim
Now falls where warm brown horses
Will not tread again.

Kathleen McCallum

THE LOST LAND OF LYONESSE

I DREAMED, I dreamed of Lyonesse
And saw the fabled cities there;
The fields and vineyards yielding plenty,
A people richly clothed and fair.

It was a land of many churches,
Soaring spires and sacred wells,
Flowering courtyards, fruits in season,
And high above the singing bells —

Chiming carillons of music
On the clear, grape-scented air;
It touched the shuttered sun-washed houses;
The laughing children in the square.

Then the golden cities darkened,
The wind in fury raged and roared,
Rent the spires and all before it;
Through sleeping streets the water poured.

The broken bells were rolling, tolling,
I heard the lost souls cry and call;
Saw Trevelyan, white steed thundering
From towering seas, devouring all.

Still, I hear them, those bells ringing
When the wind moans wild and free
Across the riven cliffs of granite
To land that dreams beneath the sea.

Kathryn L. Garrod

SEA DREAMS

COME aboard our gallant dream ship;
　　She's a galleon, not a steamship,
E'er she bids farewell to harbour
In the sunset glow.
With an offshore breeze a-blowing,
And an ebb-tide strongly flowing,
She'll be on her way to dreamland
Just as soon as she can go.

Fast she flies and ever faster,
For the night wind is her master;
See the canvas stretching tautly
And the bending of the spars.
To the watch bell's silver ringing
How the crew is sweetly singing,
'Neath an endless shawl of sable
Sequinned by a trillion stars.

Now a town's spread out before us!
Loud the sailors' joyful chorus!
Shrill the gulls cry out a welcome
As the pale moon gleams.
Spires and domes rise up to meet us,
We'll have smiling lips to greet us,
While our vessel rides at anchor
In the harbour of our dreams.

Peter Cliffe

AUTUMN STARLINGS

TODAY I woke to a lovely sound,
The beat of wings was all around,
Swooping, darting wings in flight,
I gazed in gladness and delight.
There, where the Autumn sun hung low,
Alighting swiftly on tiptoe,
Frolicking, frisking, full of glee,
A flutter of birds in the elder tree.

The leaves were shining all aglow,
The boughs were swaying to and fro
On laden branches, berries sweet
Shook to the touch of tiny feet,
In that jostling jamboree
Of starlings in the elder tree.
God gave me flowers the Summer through,
The Autumn fruit I give to you.

Eileen Melrose

THE BULB CATALOGUE

LETTERS to be written, bills to be paid,
　　Lists to be checked and estimates made,
Telephone to answer, telegrams to send,
Money to be borrowed (but refuse to lend!)
Typewriters rattling all in a row,
Sign the forms, stamp the chits, then away they go.
Tear up the circulars, toss the postcards by,
Pitch them in the basket, let the fragments lie.
Ah, here's a bulb list! Snatch a stolen moment;
Flick the pages over and see what's in it . . .

I remember crocuses; a Springtime long ago,
In pastures of high Lombardy, streaked with melting snow,
Where through the bleached and wintry grass the shining freshets run,
And lean, rough-coated cattle graze and dawdle in the sun;
And, massed in glowing companies to greet the Spring, their Lord,
The golden crocus-torches flame triumphant from the sward.

I remember Rydal, a pearl among the hills,
Where all along the water's edge dance Wordsworth's daffodils;
Fair and aureoled angel heads, nodding as they lean
Above the silver ripples and among the bladed green;
Surely they still dream of him, remember it was he,
Whose lovely, loving poem, is their immortality . . .

Slam the door on memory, put temptation by,
Working days are not for dreams, fast the minutes fly;
Throw the catalogue away, drive the scribbling pen,
Turn from flowery reverie to weary world of men.
Yet each garish picture, every coloured word
Has set my heart a-singing, singing, singing like a bird.

M. L. Dalgleish

SERENADE
TO SQUIRRELS

SQUIRRELS in the tree tops,
   Flying through the air,
Squirrels in the garden,
Squirrels everywhere.

They scamper through the woodland,
And creep along the fence,
Climb swiftly up high tree trunks,
Food hunting, so intense.

Frustrated over bird food,
Caged neatly out of reach,
For nuts they strive and struggle,
And hang on like a leech.

Then in traditional poses,
They nibble seeds and such,
And look so sweet and pretty,
I love them very much.

Although they eat the blossoms,
And nip camellia heads,
In spite of vicious history
Of killing all the reds;

I love their frisky manner,
Their tails flashed through with white,
Their playful, cute behaviour,
As they race out of sight.

Some call them pests, a nuisance,
As they live wild and free,
But I know that I'd miss them,
If they didn't live with me.

Chrissy Greenslade

HAME-SWEET-HAME

SITTIN' by the fireside
On a Winter's afternoon
Wi' the coals heaped up the chimney
'Til you're almost in a swoon,
An' you feel your head grow heavy
An' you feel your eyelids droop
'Cause your stomach's fu' tae burstin'
Wi' a plate o' hame-made soup!

Happy by the fireside
Wi' the cat upon yer lap
An' he's havin' forty winks
So you think you'll tak' a nap,
An' his whiskers are a' milky
An' he's purrin' at the heat
An' he's workin' oot while sleepin'
How tae pinch yer favourite seat!

Dozin' by the fireside
Wi' the dugs doon at yer feet
Wi' paws and tails a' twitchin'
As they rin the rabbit-beat,
Wi' one ear cocked for danger
An' the ither cocked fur grub
An' noses at the ready
Tae receive a frien'ly rub!

Cosy by the fireside
Wi' a bairnie on yer knee
Of a' the places in the world
Why that's the place tae be,
For of a' the pleasures known tae man
There's ane that stays the same
Sittin' by the fireside —
In yer hame — sweet — hame!

Fiona Walker

A HUSBAND WITH THE FLU

HAVE you ever had a husband with the flu?
  If you have you'll know exactly what to do.
You'll hold his sweaty hand
Showing that you understand,
Then listen to his groans and moaning, too.

He'll tell you how he hates to be complaining,
But if you only knew how he is paining.
He says he's nearly dying
And even though he's lying,
You'll not let on you really know he's feigning.

He now knows he has all of your attention
And you'll listen to each thing he has to mention;
His aching eyes and burning throat,
His tongue which has a furry coat,
And how he'll have to miss the firm's convention.

Well, a man has much to do most of his life
To earn a living, handle stress and strife;
Though it's sometimes hard to see,
He needs all the sympathy
From his better half; a loving mum and wife.

Lola Lingard

BEACHED

GREY old sailorman, down by the shore,
    Where the in-rolling waves are gleaming,
Filling the air with the shingle's roar,
Why do you stand there dreaming?

Do you still remember the golden lights
Of the little old shanty town,
And the perfumed heat of the tropic nights,
And the maidens so slim and brown?

Or is it the ocean that calls you still,
Its thoughts of a long haul bringing;
The bite of the wind, so strong and chill,
And the albatross silently winging?

It's all in the past, old man of the sea,
Who watches the great waves creaming.
Just dream of the days that used to be,
To the sound of the wild gulls screaming.

Peter Cliffe

OLD TIN MINES
— ST AGNES

BROODING and gaunt against the sky,
   Lone sentinels stand proudly by,
Monuments left by men of toil,
Mining deep beneath Cornish soil.

On hills and rugged cliff outlie,
Broken fingers pointing high;
Echoes of engine's thump and whine,
Pumping below Wheel Kitty mine.

Wind-swept granite still defy
As gorse and ivy dignify,
Darkness and dirt of brutal graft,
Working the tin of Sara's shaft.

Seagulls cruise with watchful eye,
Ghosts of the past their mournful cry;
No noise of men, machines at toil,
Silence, beneath old Cornish soil.

Kathryn L. Garrod

FIRST FROST

COLD is the night,
    The moon upon the river silver-bright,
Black shadows on the ben,
And cottage lights that waken, one by one,
Along the silent glen.

Sharp is the air,
The frosty moorland grasses, stiff and spare,
Crackle beneath the heel,
And pools that held the sun's reflected fire
To sheets of ice congeal.

Dark are the trees,
The ancient forest full of mysteries,
Moonlight and shadow-bars.
Above, the vault of Heaven, darkly-blue,
Is strewn with brilliant stars.

Brenda G. Macrow

WINTER NIGHTS

WINTER with her magic wand
    Has sparkled all the trees,
Has touched each branch with silver
And caused the streams to freeze.

Jack Frost on every window
Has turned the panes opaque,
And roofs lie, white and pristine
Like the icing on a cake.

The fields, which yesterday were brown
Now sleep beneath the snow,
And though it's only four o'clock
It's time for lamps to glow.

Time now to curl beside the fire
With tea and buttered toast,
To write a friendly letter
To catch the morning post.

Time, too, to look into the flames
With tranquil, pensive stare,
And see the dancing pictures
Which are reflected there.

To dream of Christmas coming
With all its warmth and cheer,
And of the earth's awakening
In the Springtime of the year.

Fiona Walker

TRUST

FIVE days the snow had lain
    Deep as a boot. Mouths of ice
Hung from roofs and windows,
The river slid by like a wolf.

At noon I went out with crumbs
Cupped in one hand. As I crouched,
A robin fluttered from nowhere,
Grasped the landfall of my palm.

A rowan eye inspected me
Side on. The blood-red throat
Swelled and sank, breathing quickly,
Till hungry, the beak stabbed fast.

The robin finished, turned,
Let out one jewel of sound
Then ruffled up into the sky —
A skate on the frosty air.

Kenneth C. Steven

The artists are:—

Sheila Carmichael; When . . ., Winter Nights.
Jackie Cartwright; The Visitor, The Thoroughbred, Serenade To Squirrels.
John Dugan; Song: O Mary MacNeil, The Call Of The Band, Sea Dreams.
Allan Haldane; Oh, Avalon!, Vagabond, The Fiddler At The Gate, The Bulb Catalogue.
Eunice Harvey; Waiting, A Night In June, Summer Magic, A Husband With The Flu.
Harry McGregor; Home Thoughts From Barbados, Remembering You, The Window, Summer Pilgrimage, The Lost Land Of Lyonesse.
John Mackay; Rebecca Dancing, Ballad.
Sandy Milligan; Ma Petite, Haresfield, Helter-Skelter, Hame-Sweet-Hame.
Keith Robson; Grantham, Dry-stone Dykers, The Cloisters – Gloucester Cathedral, Hill Farm, Old Tin Mine – St Agnes.
Staff Artists; My Feathered Friends, Breath Of Winter, Sorry, The Day That Was, Fairyland, The Rainbow, Spring Fever, Tomorrow's Promise, Upstairs On The Bus, The Patchwork Quilt, Mull, Windsurfers, Reflections, Our Cathy And Me, Autumn Starlings, Beached, First Frost, Trust.

JULY

S	M	T	W	T	F	S
			1	2	3	4
5	6	7	8	9	10	11
12	13	14	15	16	17	18
19	20	21	22	23	24	25
26	27	28	29	30	31	

SEPTEMBER

S	M	T	W	T	F	S
		1	2	3	4	5
6	7	8	9	10	11	12
13	14	15	16	17	18	19
20	21	22	23	24	25	26
27	28	29	30			

NOVEMBER

S	M	T	W	T	F	S
1	2	3	4	5	6	7
8	9	10	11	12	13	14
15	16	17	18	19	20	21
22	23	24	25	26	27	28
29	30					